LITTLE MISS CONTRARY

by Roger Hargreaves

EGMONT

Little Miss Contrary always did the opposite
of what you would think she would do.

For instance.

If you asked her to switch on the television, she would
switch on the light.

For example.

If you asked her the time, she would tell you the date.

And she always said the opposite of what she really
meant!

Mind you.

It wasn't exactly her fault.

It was probably because she lived in a place called Muddleland where everything is so mixed up and muddled you don't know whether you are coming or going.

Or "going or coming", as they say in Muddleland.

It's a very strange place indeed!

The worms don't live in holes in Muddleland.

They live in trees!

And the birds live in holes!

And if you want a loaf of bread you don't go to the baker's, you go to the butcher's.

The baker sells bananas!

One morning Little Miss Contrary was having breakfast.

Roast beef and Yorkshire pudding.

There was a knock at the door.

Little Miss Contrary didn't hear it at first because it was more of a tap than a knock.

Tap … tap … tap.

But she did hear it eventually, and went to see who it was.

She opened the door.

"Hello," said a little voice.

Little Miss Contrary looked down, and down again, and there stood Mr Small.

He raised his hat. "Hello," he said again.

"Goodbye," smiled Little Miss Contrary.

Mr Small looked puzzled. As well he might!

"I wonder if you can help me?" he asked.

Little Miss Contrary smiled.

"Of course I can't," she said.

"Oh dear," said Mr Small. "You see, I'm lost!"

"Well," she said, "nice to meet you, Mr Lost!"

"No! No!" said Mr Small. "I'm trying to find somebody called Little Miss Contrary!"

"That's you," laughed Little Miss Contrary.

"I have a letter for her," said Mr Small.

"Oh bad," she said, "I don't get any telephone calls!"

"I think I'll go," said the confused Mr Small. "Goodbye!"

"Hello," said Little Miss Contrary, and shut the door.

Mr Small went home, shaking his head.

The letter was from Mr Happy, inviting Little Miss Contrary to his birthday party.

Mr Happy had never met Little Miss Contrary, but he had heard about her, and thought it would be nice to have her to his party.

The invitation was for three o'clock on Tuesday March 14th.

At two o'clock on Monday March 13th Little Miss Contrary knocked on Mr Happy's door.

"Happy Christmas," said Little Miss Contrary, and thrust a parcel into Mr Happy's hands.

Mr Happy was puzzled. "Who are you?" he asked.

"I'm Little Miss Sunshine," replied Little Miss Contrary.

"No, you're not," said Mr Happy. "I know Little Miss Sunshine, and she's not a bit like you."

Then he stopped and thought.

"Oh," he smiled. "I know who you really are. You're Little Miss Contrary, aren't you? I've heard that you always say and do the opposite of what you mean!"

"You'd better come in," said Mr Happy.

"No thank you," smiled Little Miss Contrary.

Mr Happy led her into his living room.

"What a horrible room," she said.

Mr Happy grinned. He was beginning to realise that everything he had heard about Little Miss Contrary was true.

"Would you like a cup of tea?" he asked.

"I can't think of anything I'd like less," said Little Miss Contrary.

Mr Happy grinned again, and went to put the kettle on.

After his tea, Mr Happy took Little Miss Contrary to meet some of his friends.

He had to explain to them all that what she was saying was the exact opposite of what she really meant.

"Aren't you thin?" she said to Mr Greedy.

"You have very short arms!" she said to Mr Tickle.

"I like your beard!" she said to Mr Fussy.

"Well," she said eventually. "Thank you for the most perfect afternoon. Now I must go home before it gets light!"

"Perfect?" asked Mr Happy.

"Perfectly dreadful," she agreed.

And off she went.

"I say," chuckled Mr Greedy to Mr Happy, "you do know some funny people!"

"You can say that again," laughed Mr Happy.

"You do know some funny people," said Mr Greedy.

Mr Happy grinned, and went home.

At home Mr Happy remembered the parcel that Little Miss Contrary had given him.

"It must be a birthday present," he said. And he hurried to where he had left the parcel, and unwrapped it. Inside was indeed a present, and a card. He opened the birthday card first.

Inside it said, "MANY MISERABLE RETURNS OF THE DAY".

And, would you like to know what the present was?

A pair of socks.

Well.

Not quite a PAIR of socks.

One sock was white!

And the other sock was black!

And, as Little Miss Contrary would say, "that is the beginning of the story"!